"Be yourself; everyone else is taken."
Oscar Wilde

First US edition 2021

Library of Congress Catalog Card Number pending
ISBN 978-1-5362-1770-4

LEO 26 25 24 23 22 21
10 9 8 7 6 5 4 3 2 1

Printed in Heshan, Guangdong, China

This book was typeset in Stempel Schneidler.
The illustrations were done in watercolor and ink.

Candlewick Press
99 Dover Street
Somerville, Massachusetts 02144

www.candlewick.com

CANDLEWICK PRESS

Maxine

Bob Graham

Babies were born all the time in Max's neighborhood. But never had Max been told he was going to have a new baby brother or sister . . . until now!

His mom, superhero Madam Thunderbolt, hugged him in her steel-like grip while Max held his breath.

"It's right in here," she said. "Let's go to the hospital to take a picture."

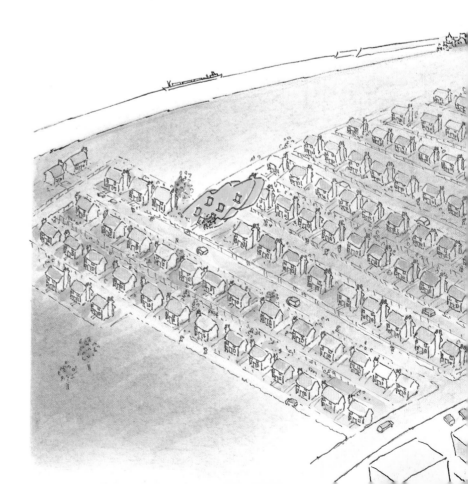

Max's dad's voice shook as he asked,
"Is it a boy or a girl?"

"It's too early to say, Captain Lightning," replied
the nurse. "But the mask is already fully formed."

"Miraculous!" exclaimed Madam Thunderbolt.

The baby arrived at the stroke of midnight along with
two little strands of red hair. She blinked.
"Let's call her Maxine," said her mom.
"Yes, Maxine!" said her brother, Max.

"Then Maxine she shall be,"
said a proud Captain Lightning.
The nurses and doctors stopped work
and they clapped.

At home, her grandma hugged her.

Her grandad kissed her.

"Such tiny little fingers.

Such a perfect little mask," they said,

then hugged her some more.

And there were presents!

A hand-knitted super cape
from Grandma.

And boots of the softest
leather from Grandad.

Max gave her his copy of
Veterinary Treatment for Animals.
"She'll be reading in no time at all,"
said Captain Lightning.

Before the superhero parents returned to work catching thieves, crooks, and bullies,

they took Maxine to show off at the office. Max went, too.

There was no crime that day,
just a missing soft toy somewhere out on the East Side.
"We'll deal with that tomorrow," said the Chief of Police.

In no time at all,
Maxine was walking.

Maxine's first words arrived together
just to keep each other company.
"Car keys," she said.

She read the whole of Max's present.
She looked at the pictures
and counted the pages, too.

Then, as expected, she flew.
And she grew!

Her clothes shrunk away from her,
like the tide going out.
Maxine started school four years early.

"Children, this is Maxine Lightning-Thunderbolt.
She may be small, but she has a lot packed into
this little head of hers," said Miss Honeyset.

"Maxine, we have another superboy.
Garth Gecko can be your buddy
and show you around."

At lunch, Maxine saw cool T-shirts
and jeans ripped just right.
Her super cape hung listless as a sail.

Blushing, she tried to hide it.
Garth was no help.
He just walked up walls.

At home, Maxine said, "Mommy, I just can't
wear these droopy things to school."
Then her voice dropped to a whisper.
"Even though Grandma made them."

"Please can I have a T-shirt and some jeans?" Maxine asked.
"Maxine! Superheroes do NOT wear jeans," her mom said.
"Kids today!" said Grandad.

"Maxine, NO Lightnings have EVER worn jeans.
No Thunderbolts either!" said her mom.
Maxine replied, "Things will always be changing, Mommy."

Madam Thunderbolt looked softly at her daughter.
The next day, they went shopping at Jeans Junction.

"These are big, with room
to grow," said the assistant.

"Or these cut nicely in the waist?
Maybe a little long in the leg?"

The third pair gripped her like
a fist. "Tight's cool," said Max.

They had a special leather patch with
the name branded with a hot poker.

"Shall I put the old clothes in a bag, Madam?"

"Yes, she can wear the new top, jeans, and shoes.

She'll keep the mask on."

"Think you'll fly without the cape, Maxi?" asked Max.

"Well, you once did," said his mom.

"That was different!" said Max.

"That was a baby bird rescue."

"No cape, Maxine?
Can you still fly?"

"I guess!"
she replied.

"You haven't tried?
Too SCARED to try?"

One finger corkscrewing in her hair, Maxine said,
"Could if I wanted! Flying's in our family . . .

and red hair, too. My great-grandma
had red hair and eyes as green as the sea."

After school, Lucy asked Maxine's grandma,
"Did you want to be a superhero when you were little?"
"Of course, I was born with a cape on," she replied.

"I'm going to be a rocket scientist," said Lucy.

"I'll be a pirate," said Aretha.

"I'll be a drummer," said Angela.

"I'm thinking deep-sea diver," said Poppi.

"I'll climb Everest," said Garth.

"It's 29,032 feet high," replied Maxine.
"That's *definitely* for you, Garth."
Then Max said, "Maxi knows these things.
She can do anything she wants."

That night, Maxine's thoughts hovered like soap bubbles.
She had answers for many things.
"But who am I going to be?" she asked out loud.
That question burst softly on the ceiling.

Upstairs, Max fixed the broken shell of a snail. He said, "The school fair is tomorrow. Are you going to be in the costume parade, Maxi?" There was silence. She frowned a little.

"No!" was all she said.

The next day, the school playground was transformed.
There was a rock band with Garth's mom on guitar
and a costume parade for the little kids.

A bake sale. "Careful with my Lightning cake, dear."

A cutest pet competition.

And Maxine's mom made a donation to the "pre-loved" clothes rack, a small tear showing from under her mask.

Suddenly Maxine took a deep breath. She headed straight for a small boy in the costume parade.

"Who are you?" she asked.

"Um . . . The Boy Marvel?"

"You seem a little unsure," answered Maxine.

"Here," she said, "you need this . . .

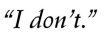

"MAXINE!"

exclaimed her family and friends.

"Exactly!" she replied.

A new Maxine! No cape.
No mask. Could she still fly?

With a little lift and push . . .

Maxine flew!

And with the cry of the birds
and the soft thump of wings on air,
Maxine and her brother, Max,
flew south across the city.